ALLISON

Allen Say

HOUGHTON MIFFLIN COMPANY ✦ BOSTON 1997

Walter Lorraine *wл* Books

Copyright © 1997 by Allen Say

Library of Congress Cataloging-in-Publication Data
Say, Allen.
    Allison / Allen Say
        p.   cm.
    Summary: When Allison realizes that she looks more like her
favorite doll than like her parents, she comes to terms with this
unwelcome discovery with the help of a stray cat.
        ISBN 0-395-85895-X
    [1. Adoption — Fiction.   2. Dolls — Fiction.   3. Cats — Fiction.]
I. Title.
PZ7.S2744A1   1997
[E] — dc21   97-7528
                                                                      CIP
                                                                       AC

Printed in the United States of America
HOR 10 9 8 7 6 5 4 3 2 1

For Yuriko

In Allison's family there were Mother, Father, Allison, and Mei Mei.

They all lived in the only house Allison had ever known.

Allison thought that Mei Mei was her little sister.

To everyone else, Mei Mei was only a doll.

So the day Grandmother sent her a package, Allison showed it first to Mei Mei.

"A dress, just like yours!" Allison held up her present.

"Meow!" Mei Mei cried.

But it wasn't the doll at all. A stray cat was looking in the window.

"Kitty," Allison called.

As she opened the door, the cat ran away.

"What a lovely kimono," Mother said.

"Kimono," Allison repeated. "Is Mei Mei's dress a kimono too?"

"Yes, but hers is very old and from far away," Father said.

"Try it on, Allison."

Mother tied the obi for her and exclaimed, "How pretty!
Look in the mirror."

Allison looked in the mirror and smiled. She saw
Mother and Father smiling over her shoulders.
She held Mei Mei next to her and saw that Mei Mei's
hair was dark and straight like hers. Allison looked
at her mother, then at her father. Her smile disappeared.

At lunchtime Allison sat quietly.

"Are you all right?" Father asked.

"Do you have a tummy ache?" Mother asked.

"Where did Mei Mei come from?" Allison asked.

"Far, far away, from another country,"
Father said. "Mommy and I went there
and brought you and Mei Mei home with us."

Allison stared. "You're not my Mommy and Daddy?"

"Of course we are," Father said. "You've been
with us since you were a little baby."

"You're the only child we have," Mother said.
"We love you very much."

"Where's my Mommy? Where's my Daddy?"
Allison cried.

9

"They didn't want me?" Allison asked.

"We're sure they wanted you but we never met
them," Mother said.

"They were not able to keep you but they wanted
you to have a mother and father," Father said.

"Can't I see a picture of them?" Allison asked.

Father shook his head.

"There was only your doll. You called her
Mei Mei even then," Mother said.

Cradling Mei Mei in her arms,
Allison went to her room.

The next morning at daycare, Allison asked Eric,

"Are your daddy's eyes like your eyes?"

Eric nodded. "They're blue," he said.

"Do you have a mommy in another country?"

"No, she's home."

"I mean another mommy who gave you away."

The children stared at Allison. She went outside.

Allison didn't climb the monkey bars.

She didn't play in the sandbox.

She didn't ride a tricycle.

She didn't play tag with Julie and Vanessa and Sean.

She didn't kick a soccer ball with Megan and Matthew.

"Come get on the merry-go-round!" Ms. Benton called.

Allison didn't answer.

In the afternoon Allison watched as the parents picked
up their children.

Mark's mother lifted him to give him a kiss.

Lori's father helped her put on her coat.

Derek pulled on his mother's arm and made her run all
the way to their car.

Kasey's grandmother talked to her in words that no one
else could understand.

"There you are," Allison's mother said, reaching down
to take her hand. Allison moved away.

On the ride home, she stared out the window
and didn't say a word.

17

Mother didn't hear a sound from Allison's room all afternoon.

Finally, she went to the door and knocked. There was no answer.

She went in.

"What have you done?" Mother cried.

"Her hair wasn't like Mei Mei's," Allison said without looking up.

Broken dolls and shredded dresses were everywhere.

"Oh, no, poor Andy! I've had him since I was a little girl."

"I don't care. You're not my mommy!" Allison exclaimed.

When Father came home from work, his face darkened.
"What have you done to my baseball and mitt?" he
shouted. "My dad gave me that mitt and now it's
all torn and the baseball's ruined."
"Dirty mitt and stupid baseball!" Allison yelled.
"You're not my daddy!" And she ran to her room.

"I'll never give you away," Allison said, stroking
Mei Mei's hair.

The doll stared back but said nothing.

Suddenly the girl sat up and cried out. "Allison
isn't my real name! Do you know what
my real name is?"

"Meow!" Mei Mei answered.

But it was only the stray cat again, looking in
from the outside.

"Don't you have a mommy?" Allison whispered.
She went to the kitchen, poured a little milk into
a saucer, and took it out into the garden. The cat
followed her with his eyes. Gently, Allison
set the saucer down and waited.
After a while the cat stole over to the dish and
lapped the milk, softly at first, then noisily,
until it was all gone. The cat looked up, licked its
mouth, and cried. Slowly, the girl reached out and
touched the cat and the cat purred.

"Look! I made friends with the kitty!" Allison called.

Mother came rushing to the door.

"Be careful! Cats have sharp claws," she said.

"He doesn't scratch. Look!" Allison lifted the cat in her arms.

"He likes you," Father said from the doorway.

"May I keep him?" Allison asked.

"He's so big. Wouldn't you rather have a nice kitten instead?"

"I want this one," Allison cried. "He doesn't have a mommy or a daddy."

"Cats chew things. He could ruin your toys," Father said.

"I won't get angry," Allison said. "I'm sorry I broke your things."

"We'll fix Andy. He'll be all right," Mother said.

"I'll have my mitt and ball bronzed like I did for your first shoes," Father said.

"But do you think the kitty wants to live with us?" Mother asked.

"Yes, he does! He likes us. He wants a home," Allison said.

"Looks like our family is getting bigger," Father said.

"He can be part of our family?" Allison asked.

"If you think he will be happy with us," Mother said.

"Yes, oh yes!" Allison cried. "He will be happy with me, with Mei Mei, with Mommy and Daddy."

"What should we call him?" Mother asked.

"A real boy's name," Father said.

"I'll have to think about it with Mei Mei," Allison said.

"Meow!" the cat cried.

Everyone laughed.

The stray cat wasn't a stray anymore.

31